John and Dickens

John and Dickens
A Christmas Mystery

a novella
by
John Passfield

Rock's Mills Press
Rock's Mills, Ontario • Oakville, Ontario
2023

Published by
Rock's Mills Press
www.rocksmillspress.com

Cover design: Craig Passfield
Cover illustration: Dickens in his chair: A play on "Dickens's Dream" by
Robert William Buss (1875), with a sketch of Dickens by Charles Martin
(1844) and block-and-circle drawings by John Passfield.

For information about this book, including bulk and retail orders and permis-
sions requests, please contact the publisher:
customer.service@rocksmillspress.com

Author's website: www.johnpassfield.ca

John and Dickens

Chapter 1

Looking out the window. Snow on the car and on the grass and on the trees. A few weeks into December. Winter boots and winter coat and winter hat.

Fellow-passengers to the grave.

I like to get up early. Wait for sunrise to light up the land. Read for a while if it's still too early to go. An every-December ritual. Stroll along the beach at Port Maitland. It's sure to be windy and cold, but I'll be okay. I walk along the beach in December every year. Dress properly and you can even enjoy the cold.

Two people

A man going for a coffee-drive.
A river with plenty of open ice.
A ritual that is performed at Christmas-time.

approached each other

What is special for you about Christmas?
How many Christmases have you known?
Does any one of your Christmases rank above them all?

in the middle of a desert.

How much is conveyed in those two short words.
How many tales of distress and misery.
Broken fortunes and ruined hopes.

Driving through the coffee line-up. White clouds of exhaust from all the cars. Made sure the window wasn't frozen shut before I left home. Just a coffee and a dash of milk is all I need.
The light of early day.
Writing-bag on the seat beside me. Reading glasses, paper and pen. I'll sip my coffee and do some polishing before I return.

A boy was born in Blunderstone, Suffolk.

"Dickens has often been compared to Shakespeare for his power of effortless invention, his brilliant play of language, the scope and density of his imagined world."
"Dickens requires us to re-examine most of our conceptions of what a novel should be."

Driving down to Port Maitland.
Driving down to Lake Erie.

A shipwrecked sailor
was struggling
in the water.

I'll be okay - have to figure out - what an amazing treat - knew exactly what he wanted - a restless throng of beings - new field of exploration - huddle under a blanket - that is the case - a life-long reader - take further precautions.

Marley was dead: to begin with. There is no doubt whatever about that. The register of his burial was signed by the clergyman, the clerk, the undertaker, and the chief mourner. Scrooge signed it: and Scrooge's name was good upon 'Change, for anything he chose to put his hand to. Old Marley was as dead as a door-nail.

Mind! I don't mean to say that I know, of my own knowledge, what there is particularly dead about a door-nail. I might have been inclined, myself, to regard a coffin-nail as the deadest piece of ironmongery in the trade. But the wisdom of our ancestors is in the simile; and my unhallowed hands shall not disturb it, or the Country's done for. You will therefore permit me to repeat, emphatically, that Marley was as dead as a door-nail.

They're grapes –
just grapes,
said the one.

Driving down to Lake Erie. Following the highway along the Grand. Patches of ice and open water. Hasn't been a cold December. Should be plenty of open ice in the lake near where I park the car.
The brisk fire of questioning.
We used to go down to the cottage sometime every December. Just to check on things and see how high the ice was piled up on the shore. We always bundled up warm just in case.
Everything could yield him pleasure.
December and Dickens – Dickens and December. Dickens is a very intriguing character. It would be in-

teresting to get to talk to him. I'd like to ask him about the mystery of Edwin Drood.

The louring houses gossiped
as he walked along the street.

A boy was placed in the window of a blacking factory.

He had a way
of facing the daylight.

Unrelieved wretchedness and successful knavery.
Just manages to live from hand to mouth.
Barely sufficient to satisfy the present cravings.

Ice frozen solid in the harbour. Ice in piles on the beach. Patches of sand kept clean, here and there, by the wind and the waves. I won't have any trouble doing what I want to do.

The groping and floundering condition.

It's just a simple ritual. Take a jagged stone from our driveway. Take it down to Lake Erie. Look for an open spot in the ice and throw it into the lake.

A boy was born in the marsh country, within twenty miles of the sea.

"Each element of the Dickens pattern is extremely simple."

"A multiplicity of simplistic elements is superimposed, one over another, making up the complexity of Dickens's art."

Walking along the frozen beach.

A jagged stone and a cup of coffee in my hands.

Amid the debris
of the wreck
he spied a book.

Do some polishing - a balanced aspect of myself -
see behind the scenes - couldn't replenish it - his reflect-
ed face - on the surface - two vagabonds - ask me any-
thing - began to flow upstream - tugging the other way.

Scrooge knew he was dead? Of course he did. How could it be otherwise? Scrooge and he were partners for I don't know how many years. Scrooge was his sole executor, his sole administrator, his sole assign, his sole residuary legatee, his sole friend, and sole mourner. And even Scrooge was not so dreadfully cut up by the sad event, but that he was an excellent man of business on the very day of the funeral, and solemnised it with an undoubted bargain.

The mention of Marley's funeral brings me back to the point I started from. There is no doubt that Marley was dead. This must be distinctly understood, or nothing wonderful can come of the story I am going to relate. If we were not perfectly convinced that Hamlet's Father died before the play began, there would be nothing more remarkable in his taking a stroll at night, in an easterly wind, upon his own ramparts, than there would be in any other middle-aged gentleman rashly turning out after dark in a breezy spot – say Saint Paul's Churchyard for instance – literally to astonish his son's weak mind.

When he was outside-out
and inside-in,
everyone knew him.

Out of the car and walking. Collar pulled up and toque pulled down. Hills of ice on the edge of the beach but I can throw overtop of the piles.
The satisfaction of thinking.
December and Dickens – Dickens and December. Thoughts of Dickens just won't go away. The man who some people say invented Christmas cheer.

It was a story

A landscape covered in snow.
Thoughts about the meaning of a Christmas book.
Two people meeting in a desert.

in search

Was Christmas better when you were a boy?
Is Christmas better now you are old?
Is Christmas better as experienced in life or as read in a book?

of an author.

Looking at the water – calm today. The same water that pounds the lighthouse in a storm. Clutching the jagged stone tightly in my hand. I rear back and throw it as far out over the water as I can.
Let us have no meanderings.
My wife is decorating the house today. All the Christmas memorabilia that we have collected over

the years. She kept every work of art that our kids ever made. I brought the boxes up from the basement and put them in the rooms and in the hall. She does this every year. She knows where every memento and keep-sake always goes.

Chapter 2

What in the world is this? This is quite an amazing scene. I know exactly what it is, though – you can't fool me. It's Charles Dickens – I'm sure it is. He's seated on a chair – surrounded by his characters. No one says a word. I guess they're all surprised to be looking at me. I recognize some of them – Oliver – Nancy – Mr. Pickwick – though it's been a long time since I read their books. I've watched a number of the movies over the years, but these aren't actors – these are the real people – the real characters – the real Dickens personae – the characters that he created – as real as me. And here they are – all gathered around his chair.

Mentally introduced himself.

Hello, Mr. Dickens. My name is John. I don't know how I got here. Or why. Though I'm interested in your books – your stories – your works. I'm – well – actually, I'm a Canadian – though my mother was from Kent. Ospringe, in Kent. Near Faversham. I live in Canada – not far from Niagara Falls.

Each had found himself

A man who finds himself in a fictional world.
A face on a knocker on a door.
A community which is counting on a legend.

making his way

What questions would you want to ask of Charles Dickens?
What could he possibly add to what he has written?
Wouldn't all of your questions be answered by his books?

in a sign-less land.

The first day of light.
Illuminates the gloom.
Converting obscurity into dazzling brilliancy.

The witch paced back and forth. She had worn a deep groove in the floor of her cave. Every hour she turned the hourglass upside down.
A disputed question.
No need to explain, John. No need, at all, to explain. I know all about you. Where you come from and why you are here. I know more than you yourself could possibly know. Actually, I am the one who is able to explain to you. You see, John – I created you. I am going to make plans for you. You are an imaginary creation – one of the characters with whom I people my imaginary tales. You are an idea that has just occurred to me.
Possessed of no facts.
The characters are gathered around Dickens. This is such an amazing scene. But it's almost deja-vu, because – well – though I haven't been in this room, I sense that my eyes have seen all this before. I'm sure there's a famous painting – or a drawing – or a sketch – of a similar scene. And I certainly know some of the Dickens-char-

acters – though for others, I couldn't possibly attach a name. Sam Weller – Mr. Brownlow – Mr. Jingle. When they talk, I'll remember the voices – the way the voices are written in print – in Dickens, each character talks in a way that's quite unique. Dickens seems to be quite voluble – he's even telling me who I am – but – so far at least – not one of these people – these characters – has said a word.

He was born on a Friday, at twelve o'clock at night.

"Dickens used to lock himself in his study during a period of extreme concentration which he referred to as 'the agonies of plotting and contriving a new book'."
"Dickens said that if he were not to shut himself up, obstinately and sullenly, in his room for a great many days without writing a word, he didn't think that he ever should be able to make a beginning."

I am a bird in the depths of the ocean! I am a fish on the currents of the air! I am buffeted by each gust and wave!

Finding myself in the presence of Charles Dickens. Dickens and the characters from his books.

My lungs fill up with water! My gills fill up with air! I don't think I will ever get back home!

The scope and density - dealing with an ocean - counting on a legend - no better answer ready - a fictional, fictional world - nothing to do with me - the glow of a brilliant dazzle - my infant tongue - acts as a kind of deity - complexity of presentation.

Scrooge never painted out Old Marley's name. There it stood, years afterwards, above the warehouse door: Scrooge and Marley. The firm was known as Scrooge and Marley. Sometimes people new to the business called Scrooge Scrooge, and sometimes Marley, but he answered to both names. It was all the same to him.

Oh! But he was a tight-fisted hand at the grindstone, Scrooge! a squeezing, wrenching, grasping, scraping, clutching, covetous, old sinner! Hard and sharp as flint, from which no steel had ever struck out generous fire; secret, and self-contained, and solitary as an oyster. The cold within him froze his old features, nipped his pointed nose, shrivelled his cheek, stiffened his gait; made his eyes red, his thin lips blue; and spoke out shrewdly in his grating voice. A frosty rime was on his head, and on his eyebrows, and his wiry chin. He carried his own low temperature always about with him; he iced his office in the dog-days; and didn't thaw it one degree at Christmas.

> *They're not grapes –*
> *they're wine,*
> *said the other.*

Niagara Falls – of course, of course. I was there, John – I was there. And that is where you come from, as you say. I was there on my American tour. I breathed a sigh of relief when I reached Canada, I'll have you know. The people there were so – accommodating – you see. You are my first Canadian character, John. I look forward to our acquaintance. Bye and bye, I'm sure, I'll imagine a story for you.

A disagreeable consciousness.

Dickens seems quite welcoming – even eager to have me aboard. No one else seems to accept my presence. Perhaps I've intruded into their space. The Dickens world is nothing if not exuberant. This is quiet – almost serene. Can't say that it's not what I expected, as I didn't expect anything at all. I guess it's not what I would have imagined – say if I were writing this scene. Mr. Winkle – the Artful Dodger – Mrs. Bardell. I don't see any Christmas-Carol characters. It's not a cheerful Christmas gathering, that's for sure. Why would Dickens say – or think – that he created me? And why would the other Dickens-characters – my fellows, as it were – seem leery of me?

The fatherless little stranger.

Not far from Niagara Falls – well, well, well, well, well. That explains your origin, John, for me. Not far from the cataract, I assume. Canadian by birth – with all that nationality entails. Of course, John, this explains the origin of the idea – the idea of you as it came to me. It was there that I was able to breathe fresh air. On my travels – on my journey – on my voyage – on my tour. I have made myself a Canadian. It might seem that I have conjured you out of nothing – as people assume that I do with all my characters – but I have conjured you out of more than simply air.

*They knew everything about him
it would seem.*

All day he pasted labels on blacking bottles.

He always dreaded

opening the door.

Derived from the perusal.
Careful attention, indefatigable assiduity and nice discrimination.
Search among the multifarious documents.

I have to figure out what happened. If I don't, I can't go on. It was a week since she had attempted to cast a spell.

Gropes his way.

A balanced aspect of myself, John – as all my characters are myself – but a grounded character to oversee my affairs. A Canadian! – the very person that I – or a part of me, at least – would like to be. A Canadian! – a Canadian! – what more down-to-earth sound could there be than the sound of that word? You are me – an aspect of me – of course you are. You are an aspect of me that I have always felt – felt the absence of, that is – felt as a lack. You are a calmer, more settled, more balanced, more objective – more Canadian – me.

Two distinct and separate phases.

So – welcome on the voyage, John. Feel free to offer advice. I am dealing with an ocean of concerns. I have a cast of recalcitrant creatures – for this tale that I have on the go. Every one of them is an aspect of me – me – me. I must harpoon them one by one and gaff them into the boat. You'll be my life-line, John, on this voyage. I shall give you a character-tour. You shall keep me from going overboard in the fog.

He never saw his father or his mother.

"Dickens presents the nightmare of what we are

and what we want in its most elemental and undiffer-
entiated form."

"Dickens presents what might be called the honesty
of the dream world."

I am standing in a puddle! On the brink of a mighty
falls! If I should lose my footing I will fall!

Wondering why I am seeing this scene.
Wondering why I am in this scene.

The tears form on my eyelids! My cheeks are riv-
ulets of despair! If the puddle gets much deeper, I shall
drown!

*Most of our conceptions - a cast of recalcitrant
characters - a calming presence - loud cracks on the
outer-door - turned him upside down - not willing to
analyze - root out everything else - a presence of some
sort - controlling the experience - he wrote it clearly.*

External heat and cold had little influence on
Scrooge. No warmth could warm, no wintry weather
chill him. No wind that blew was bitterer than he, no
falling snow was more intent upon its purpose, no pelt-
ing rain less open to entreaty. Foul weather didn't know
where to have him. The heaviest rain, and snow, and
hail, and sleet, could boast of the advantage over him in
only one respect. They often "came down" handsomely,
and Scrooge never did.

Nobody ever stopped him in the street to say, with
gladsome looks, "My dear Scrooge, how are you?
When will you come to see me?" No beggars implored

him to bestow a trifle, no children asked him what it was o'clock, no man or woman ever once in all his life inquired the way to such and such a place, of Scrooge. Even the blind men's dogs appeared to know him; and when they saw him coming on, would tug their owners into doorways and up courts; and then would wag their tails as though they said, "No eye at all is better than an evil eye, dark master!"

When he was inside-out
and outside-in,
no one knew him.

Not one character is as tall as Dickens. And he was not – is not – a particularly tall man. They're all beneath the level of his head – and he is seated on a chair. Not much movement as Dickens speaks – all are standing – all are looking – not at Dickens, but at me. They all seem rather – retiring – rather reticent – rather leery, perhaps of me, though some of them are quite aggressive – quite assertive – quite domineering – in their real lives – their stories – their tales. Bill Sykes – Pumblechook – Sairey Gamp. I read a lot of Dickens in my twenties – most of the novels and the biographies and the books about the books. Every critic had a theory – gave you the story behind the story – what all of it means. The last few days, I've been skimming *A Christmas Carol* – it's my Dickens-December read. I think I'll take advantage of the opportunity – ask him about his writing process – ask him to give me a glimpse of his workshop – show me how he comes up with the words that dance on the page.

A matter of considerable doubt.

I cannot explain how this has happened, Mr. Dickens. I suddenly find myself standing in this room. I know exactly where I am and who I am seeing. You and your characters are known throughout the world. It's certainly a pleasure to meet you, I assure you. I have read a number of your books. I never expected to meet one so illustrious as yourself.

This Dickens is quite a character. He seems to be making a rather odd joke. He almost took me by surprise, but he didn't quite manage to overturn the boat. I said very little before he claimed that he knew who I was. In fact, I barely got to speak before he replied. I don't think I said much more than 'Niagara Falls'. After that, he took the initiative – took the narrative and ran away. He's saying that he created me, but I wonder why.

A man was perched on a rock.
He had been stranded in a storm when his ship went down.

It wanted its story

A person who is forced to return to the underworld.
A juggler spinning gold-painted stones.
A person who is the hero of his own life.

to be told

What is the relationship between Dickens and his characters?
What is the relationship between Dickens and his books?
Is Dickens different from other authors or the same?

in its ideal form.

She had looked deep – deep – into a pair of human eyes. All the black blood rushed to her head and deserted her heart. It was the human who had cast the greater spell.

Their places are a blank.

Of course I know that Dickens has not created me, but why would he think so? I'm not at all like a Dickens character, that's for sure. There's nothing extreme and nothing eccentric about me. I wish I had a mirror – what does he see when he looks at me? Does he realize that I am not a Canadian of 1843? Does he actually believe what he says? Should I insist that I am not a creature of his imagination? Should I try to make him realize that I am me?

Chapter 3

Well – this is a cheerful, happy family. Obviously middle class. What seems to be an apartment or a suite of rooms. Something to do with Dickens – that's the point of this whole exercise. But there's no Dickens along to guide me. He said that there would be a tour. I didn't get the idea that I would be guiding myself.

Something strange, not belonging to yourself.

You are a character-in-process, John. I am working on you now. You are a character who I am in the process of creating – out of many bits and pieces, I assume. My visit to Canada – your nearness, as you said, to Niagara Falls – my sense of the Canadian character – borne out by the kind of person you seem to be. I have had a nagging irritant for the last couple of years. I have created you as an antidote – an operative counter-force – for what I would call an occupational disease.

Each wondered

A scene of a family in a room.
A person who is a character in a book.
A body of water flowing in reverse.

whether the other

Where does a book go when it has been read?
Other, of course, than back on the shelf?
Does it settle down in the deepest depths of the mind?

might be someone he knew.

Public buildings in a certain town.
Prudent to refrain from mentioning.
I will assign no fictitious name.

I am fully aware of what is happening, John. And it is a pleasure to be able to explain it to you. You are a character who I have created for a reason – who I have conjured out of the fragments of my memories and of my needs. I need you to be a counterweight of sorts, John – a second self – a wiser older-brother, to me – to bolster tendencies in me which need encouragement – support. You are a door, John – a door and also, a key.
The fog and darkness thickened.
The map was spread out on the table. On the desk, a spinning globe. All around there was nothing but chaos. Endless void on endless void.

It was predicted that he would be unlucky in life.

"The point of view in a Dickens novel is often hallucinated, fearful and insecure."
"The reader experiences the point of view of an ill-fed child."

Listening to Dickens explain my origin and my purpose.
He knows exactly what he wants me to be.

He knew exactly what he wanted.
He wrote it clearly in his will.
He wanted his unfinished book to be published.
Each with a bottle of ink and a quill.

No doubt whatsoever - an amazing scene - make my case - with his double or with his opposite - each tedious minute - quite an intriguing thought - what you stand for - would be empty pages - add to your agony - overthrows the brain.

But what did Scrooge care! It was the very thing he liked. To edge his way along the crowded paths of life, warning all human sympathy to keep its distance, was what the knowing ones call "nuts" to Scrooge.

Once upon a time – of all the good days in the year, on Christmas Eve – old Scrooge sat busy in his counting-house. It was cold, bleak, biting weather: foggy withal: and he could hear the people in the court outside, go wheezing up and down, beating their hands upon their breasts, and stamping their feet upon the pavement stones to warm them. The city clocks had only just gone three, but it was quite dark already – it had not been light all day – and candles were flaring in the windows of the neighbouring offices, like ruddy smears upon the palpable brown air. The fog came pouring in at every chink and keyhole, and was so dense without, that although the court was of the narrowest, the houses opposite were mere phantoms. To see the dingy cloud come drooping down, obscuring everything, one might have thought that Nature lived hard by, and was brewing on a large scale.

They are grapes
when they are grapes,

A man, a woman, a boy. About ten or eleven years old. Some younger children play with their toys on the rug. The boy must be Charles Dickens. But why wouldn't Dickens be here to tell me who they are? The boy sits at the table – reading a book and making notes. The man sits at the other end and stares at what must be his wallet – or his billfold – or his purse. The woman stirs the soup. The children play with their toys on the rug. Is this apartment – this family – this scene – a part of the promised tour? If it is, why would Dickens not be here?

Lonely darkness over an unknown abyss.

This is forever happening, John. I create a cast of characters. I do so for every book. I imagine them to be as alive as are you or me. I make them as independent-ly-minded as I can. And then, the inevitable happens. They all have minds, John – minds, of course – but minds, John, minds, alas, of their own. They don't always want to do what I want them to do.

There was nowhere he could turn
where he wasn't known.

People gathered on the street in front of the window.

He had a closet
that was filled with clothing.

On a day and a date.

Need not trouble myself to repeat.
It can be of no possible consequence.

I am attempting to write a book, John. A very simple Christmas-book. But writing is not an easy task, I assure you – long or short – at any time. I have had troubles in the past, John – pressing deadlines – difficult publishers – money worries and all the rest – but I've never had the problems that I am encountering now.

Must have some hidden purpose.

I can make this in one week. In fact, I can do it in six days. On the seventh, I'll take my rest. Everything will be in motion by that time.

All he knew of his family was their tombstones.

"Dickens's genius for compression, his ability to spring an entire character from a single image, results in a prose of extraordinary concentration."

"It is a prose of such suggestiveness, compact and sure of stroke, that the language itself seems an organ of perception."

Watching a scene which must be of Dickens's childhood.

Wondering whether he is showing it to me.

He sat down to write a novel.
It would be his masterpiece.
It would be a murder-mystery.
It would be a challenging read.

Of my own knowledge - recognize some of them - knew exactly what he wanted - waiting in the harbour

- still can't see myself - stands as a model - lying in wait - an author is compelled - one lingering question - not quite adequate.

The door of Scrooge's counting-house was open that he might keep his eye upon his clerk, who in a dismal little cell beyond, a sort of tank, was copying letters. Scrooge had a very small fire, but the clerk's fire was so very much smaller that it looked like one coal. But he couldn't replenish it, for Scrooge kept the coal-box in his own room; and so surely as the clerk came in with the shovel, the master predicted that it would be necessary for them to part. Wherefore the clerk put on his white comforter, and tried to warm himself at the candle; in which effort, not being a man of a strong imagination, he failed.

"A merry Christmas, uncle! God save you!" cried a cheerful voice. It was the voice of Scrooge's nephew, who came upon him so quickly that this was the first intimation he had of his approach.

"Bah!" said Scrooge, "Humbug!"

He had so heated himself with rapid walking in the fog and frost, this nephew of Scrooge's, that he was all in a glow; his face was ruddy and handsome; his eyes sparkled, and his breath smoked again.

"Christmas a humbug, uncle!" said Scrooge's nephew. "You don't mean that, I am sure?"

"I do," said Scrooge. "Merry Christmas! What right have you to be merry? What reason have you to be merry? You're poor enough."

"Come, then," returned the nephew gaily. "What right have you to be dismal? What reason have you to be morose? You're rich enough."

Scrooge having no better answer ready on the spur of the moment, said, "Bah!" again; and followed it up with "Humbug."

*When he was outside-out
and inside-in,
no one knew him.*

The same family – the same apartment – all the same people as before. The boy is reading and note-making – the mother is stirring the soup – the children are playing with their toys on the floor. The man – Dickens's father? – is paddling with his fingers inside his wallet – or his billfold – or his purse. Suddenly – everyone jumps! A loud crash! – almost like thunder! A series of loud cracks on the outer-door! The man looks at the woman – the woman looks at the boy – the boy tears his eyes away from his parents and looks at the door. Three loud cracks again! – like cracks of thunder out in the hall! The children huddle around the mother. The boy looks at the father – the father looks at the boy. The boy gets up from his book and walks across the room and opens the door.

A corner whence there was no escape.

I appreciate your willingness, Mr. Dickens, to let me see your working methods. I have always been intrigued by the question of how writers go about creating their books. Just to see a writer at work – in his workshop, as it were – is to be the recipient of a privilege that is granted to very few.

Am I showing these scenes to myself? If so, why would I bother? I already know what these scenes mean to Dickens. They're explained in all the books. He left a complete and clear explanation behind when he died. This is a mystery – an enigma – a conundrum – a puzzle. These scenes are images – they are of Dickens – they have been buried for fifty years in the depths of my mind. But what's their origin at the moment? Who is presenting these images now? Do these scenes still belong to Dickens or belong to me?

It was a rock, not an island, so there was nothing to eat or to drink.
All he had were some provisions from the wreck.

Not just any author

The beating of a heart inside a book.
A person picking another person's pocket.
A boy singing a carol through a key-hole.

would do

What is the process of image-creation?
On the ocean-floor of the mind?
What is the purpose of all that turmoil underground?

for the telling of its tale.

Where does he think this fiction will take him? Am I a handy dues ex machina who happened to drop in from the sky? – a character who he can utilize to advance some mysterious design? Maybe I shouldn't have let it happen – still, it hasn't quite happened yet. Dickens is certainly a whirlwind – a force of nature – a mother hen. Somewhat of a friendly bully – an Iago with, no doubt, a positive purpose. At any rate, it's best that I be wary – stand on guard against a benevolent take-over of my own true self.

Must have some hidden purpose.

I shall make myself a universe. I'll make it as vast as ever I can. But even bigger – unimaginably-bigger – is the mystery that I shall make of the human mind.

Chapter 4

Look here! – look at this, John!, Dickens is saying. This is old Fezziwig, John! – a character who will be in my Christmas tale! It's a scene of country dancing – couples will dance around the room! A very unique old fellow, John – based on a man I used to know! I created him as much for the humour as for anything else! See – he is dancing with his wife. Not much of a dancer, you will agree, but there will be much that I can do with my ink and my pen. For a flame, one needs a spark – just a spark from which to raise a towering plume. See – perhaps the old fellow is tired. He has been dancing since I created him – I expected to have the story written by now. Come on along with me – let's go talk to him – let's go talk to old Fezziwig. Come on John! – follow me! Dickens plunges into the scene and I am tugged by an unknown force and in I go.

Look in vain for truth.

You're aware, John, that I am a writer – of course you are. I created you with certain – elements – and with more, of course, to come. But your book – our book, John – the one that we will create together – author and character working together, as you shall see – is for the future, John. I have other plans for the present. I want you to help me with this book that I am planning now. This time, John, I am trying something new. A shorter book – a Christmas story. Far away from anything that I have tackled heretofore.

Perhaps he'll have

Two people watching a dancing scene.
A land without a sign.
Molten gold-dust being poured into a mold.

some water to share

Is Charles Dickens your favourite author? Have you read all of his books? Have you returned to them time and again over the years?

thought each of the other.

No lady or gentleman with any claims.
Can possibly sympathize.
Without being first assured.

It was the wedding of all weddings. The prince had fallen in battle. The princess had died of the plague. The legend had said that they would wed and be happy for life.
Fought out the point between them.
It's a story about an old fellow, John – a miser – who I am calling Mr. Scrooge – Ebenezer Scrooge – whose whole life has been quite terribly misspent. Does that concept make sense – fictional sense, of course – at all, to you? He's an entirely imagined personage – exaggerated in the extreme. The kind of character whom I am known to write, of course, but I am sure that you would

agree that he doesn't sound a bit like me – or you.

It was predicted that he would see ghosts and spirits.

"A Dickens novel presents a reality that has seemingly lost all coherence."
"An alternative grid is placed over this reality – an integrated pattern which is attempting to imagine itself into being."

I am tired, but I cannot sleep! I am hungry, but I cannot eat! I am thirsty, but I cannot drink!

Listening to Dickens's plans for writing *A Christmas Carol.*
I have read a book that hasn't been written yet.

What was life like when I had no troubles? What was life like when I had no cares? What was life like when I used to be someone else?

Wisdom of our ancestors - as real as me - a nagging irritant - an improved opinion of himself - his line of sight - one gigantic eye - seizes a protective rag - was fain to grope - it's a trade-off - will be worn smooth.

"Don't be cross, uncle!" said the nephew.
"What else can I be," returned the uncle, "when I live in such a world of fools as this? Merry Christmas! Out upon merry Christmas! What's Christmas time to you but a time for paying bills without money; a time for finding yourself a year older, but not an hour richer; a time for balancing your books and having every item

in 'em through a round dozen of months presented dead against you? If I could work my will," said Scrooge indignantly, "every idiot who goes about with 'Merry Christmas' on his lips, should be boiled with his own pudding, and buried with a stake of holly through his heart. He should!"

"Uncle!" pleaded the nephew.

"Nephew!" returned the uncle sternly, "keep Christmas in your own way, and let me keep it in mine."

"Keep it!" repeated Scrooge's nephew. "But you don't keep it."

"Let me leave it alone, then," said Scrooge. "Much good may it do you! Much good it has ever done you!"

"There are many things from which I might have derived good, by which I have not profited, I dare say," returned the nephew. "Christmas among the rest. But I am sure I have always thought of Christmas time, when it has come round – apart from the veneration due to its sacred name and origin, if anything belonging to it can be apart from that – as a good time; a kind, forgiving, charitable, pleasant time; the only time I know of, in the long calendar of the year, when men and women seem by one consent to open their shut-up hearts freely, and to think of people below them as if they really were fellow-passengers to the grave, and not another race of creatures bound on other journeys. And therefore, uncle, though it has never put a scrap of gold or silver in my pocket, I believe that it has done me good, and will do me good; and I say, God bless it!"

and they are wine
when they are wine,

Of course I recognize Old Fezziwig – I know *A Christmas Carol* quite well. But the old fellow seems a bit tired – not like he is, each December, when I spend an hour or two skimming the tale. But this is the actual Fezziwig – perhaps he is usually in bed at this time. It's Christmas Eve, of course, as he dances with his wife. The fiddler, too, must be tired, for the music seems, to me, a trifle slow. Dickens strides to the centre of the dancers – I remain here on the side. Dickens calls a halt and the fiddle sags and dies. Dickens offers to do the dancing – I shall show you how it shall be done! He takes Old Fezziwig by the shoulders and bids him stand aside. Then he makes, to Old Fezziwig's wife, an elaborate bow. Dickens was talking to them, but all has gone silent all of a sudden. I can't hear the fiddle at all – it's become a scene in mime – all I can see is the animated fiddler, sawing away with his arm and his bow – at two or three times the speed that he managed before. Dickens takes hold of the little old lady – little old Mrs. Fezziwig – and whirls her around and both of his calves seem to glow. Then Dickens – as he is dancing – looks back over his shoulder and winks at old Fezziwig. Old Fezziwig's eyes are popping – this is going to be me? He watches as his author – his double – his doppleganger par extreme – whirls the love of his life around the outer-edges of the Fezziwig-world and back again. Then Dickens stops – for a moment – and points back down at his calves and laughs and winks again. Then the Dickens whirlwind spins away across the floor. Mrs. Fezziwig's face grows younger – she seems to be having the time of her life. Thoughts of running away with the author, perhaps – dancing, dancing, dancing – down the street and out of town – how could life with Old Fezziwig ever be the same? What an amazing treat this is – getting to see behind the scenes. Dickens, in person, is a much more dazzling character than the characters in his books. He oozes life! – he glows! – he illuminates the scene!

I can show you a scene or two, John. Come with me as I make my rounds. I am visiting the characters who are waiting for their story to start. I would normally have been writing by now, you see, but I have met a bit of a block. The kind of block that has never been mine – at all – in the past. Oh I can write the story all right – I have the characters and their traits – and I know what I want to happen in every stave. It's just the recalcitrance – the obstinacy – the stubbornness, you see. There's resistance among the characters. It's such a ridiculous situation, John. I am forced to negotiate with the creatures whom I – myself – have made.

The houses had watched him
as he was born.

Everyone marveled that he worked with such dexterity.

He would look deeply
into his mirror.

A great satisfaction to know.
Undoubtedly descended in a direct line.
In the very earliest times closely connected.

They were counting on the legend. Surely the legend couldn't possibly fail. The prince and princess lay side-by-side. The priest was about to pronounce them man and wife.

Of no possible consequence.

Oh I'm sure you can help me, John. That is the plan – that is the object – that is the need. A calming presence is what I seek, and what I hope, in you, I have found. Watch me as I work, John. Observe the process that I follow. See me interact with each character in his milieu. I'm sure when they get to know you, John – a Canadian – diplomatic – phlegmatic – extremely serene – you can offset some of the grating between my characters and me. I am nothing if not excitable. That is your task, John, that is your function – to be a more diplomatic me. You can reason with them, John – make my case to them, as it were – a Dickens-substitute, for the moment – in what I am sure will be a much more mellow mode.

A fearful man threatened to cut his throat.

"Extreme colour, style, and manner are at the core of Dickens's novelistic technique."
"His technique is closer to poetic drama than to that of a conventional novel."

Born without a father! Born without a mother! Born without a child who would be me!

Watching Dickens interacting with the Fezziwigs. Wondering why Dickens would need an advocate.

Giving birth to a father! Giving birth to a mother! Giving birth to a child who should be me!

Plenty of open ice - a sign-less land - an occupational disease - ostensibly, at least - a very disturbing

*sight - admitted the fact - moves him into place - noth-
ing of myself - i cannot leave - take up another label.*

The clerk in the Tank involuntarily applauded. Be-
coming immediately sensible of the impropriety, he
poked the fire, and extinguished the last frail spark for
ever.

"Let me hear another sound from you," said
Scrooge, "and you'll keep your Christmas by losing
your situation! You're quite a powerful speaker, sir," he
added, turning to his nephew. "I wonder you don't go
into Parliament."

"Don't be angry, uncle. Come! Dine with us to-morrow."

Scrooge said that he would see him – yes, indeed
he did. He went the whole length of the expression, and
said that he would see him in that extremity first.

"But why?" cried Scrooge's nephew. "Why?"

"Why did you get married?" said Scrooge.

"Because I fell in love."

"Because you fell in love!" growled Scrooge, as if
that were the only one thing in the world more ridiculous than a merry Christmas. "Good afternoon!"

"Nay, uncle, but you never came to see me before
that happened. Why give it as a reason for not coming
now?"

"Good afternoon," said Scrooge.

"I want nothing from you; I ask nothing of you;
why cannot we be friends?"

"Good afternoon," said Scrooge.

"I am sorry, with all my heart, to find you so res-
olute. We have never had any quarrel, to which I have
been a party. But I have made the trial in homage to

Christmas, and I'll keep my Christmas humour to the last. So A Merry Christmas, uncle!"

"Good afternoon!" said Scrooge.

"And A Happy New Year!"

"Good afternoon!" said Scrooge.

His nephew left the room without an angry word, notwithstanding. He stopped at the outer door to bestow the greetings of the season on the clerk, who, cold as he was, was warmer than Scrooge; for he returned them cordially.

"There's another fellow," muttered Scrooge; who overheard him: "my clerk, with fifteen shillings a week, and a wife and family, talking about a merry Christmas. I'll retire to Bedlam."

When he was inside-out
and outside-in,
everyone knew him.

This is odd – very odd. Just Dickens and the Fezziwigs. All the people who were here have faded away. Just Dickens and the Fezziwigs, talking – and they seem to be at odds. I am guessing, as it is all in mime to me. The old gentleman's face seems worried. Wrinkles appear on the two old people, which the ebullience of Dickens's dancing had melted away. Mr. Fezziwig speaks to Dickens, quite in earnest, it would seem. By her nodding, the old lady would seem to agree. I'm guessing – it's all I can do – as I cannot hear a word. Dickens, in turn, is very serious – his face takes on a troubled form. The old gentleman speaks – Dickens listens – once in a while, the elderly lady adds a few words. Dickens nods, and listens, and nods, and listens again. The two old people seem deeply troubled – extremely worried – very concerned. The comical figures of Dickens's story have been revealed – by some strange process – to be not so very comical at all.

Bolted and locked against it.

I'm amazed at your powers of concentration, Mr. Dickens. Your focus on each scene – each event – each character – is quite extreme. It's almost as if you become each character in turn.

So – old Fezziwig's not a dancer. His calves don't wink in actual life. They'll only wink when Dickens writes the scene. Is this what Dickens wants to show me? – or is this just something I'm observing on my own? I never thought of Old Fezziwig as an actual person before. Which of the two Old Fezziwigs should matter most to me? It's as if he's being transformed – distilled, it seems, by Dickens – into something – into someone – a character – a person – an entity – that is the product of a Dickens-Fezziwig brew.

The ocean was blue and placid, but dark clouds lay overhead.

The gatherings of a tropical raging storm.

So it set off

Characters of independent minds.
A person who imagines himself in another form.
A book which has disappeared from a scene.

on a journey –

Is Dickens just an entertainer?
Does he have anything valid to say?

Does he have anything more to offer than Christmas cheer?

a search for form.

The priest looked at the populace. The populace looked at the priest. The clock was about to strike midnight. Does anyone know why these two should not be wed?

Between the eye and it.

I find this whole thing rather baffling. Dickens invites me into a scene. He leaps ahead and something – some force – perhaps his willpower – pulls me in. Then, he interacts with his characters – shows the characters how to act – how the characters will be written when Dickens writes the scene. But the whole thing is silent for me – I can't hear a thing. Is it Dickens – or some other force – that is in control?

Chapter 5

The boy is reading a book. He has an inkwell and a pen. The inkwell is beside him on the stone floor. I know where this is – and I know who these people are. This is Bridewell – or Clerkenwell – and the Dickens family is in jail. No – wait – it's the Marshalsea, if memory serves. Dickens's father is in debtor's prison. He is the one – the father – who is sleeping on the wooden bench. The mother and the children are lying along the wall. A blanket is too short to cover them – the stone, I assume is cold. The boy – it has to be Dickens – squints his eyes in the candle-glow. He dips his pen in the ink and makes a note.

The explanation might lie here.

I have certain things in my life, John – elements, shall we say – in the form of memories – that haunt me night and day – that govern much of what I think and feel as I live with my family, as I interact with publishers and friends. However, these – elements – never rise to the surface in what I do or what I say. But – and here is the problem – I am aware of what no one else is – that these elements – these thoughts – these memories – these concerns – are in danger of being embodied in fictional imaginings, John – embodied in my characters and their lives. Oh, I am sure, when I think back, that this has always been the case. I am sure that story-telling is – inevitably – if one takes oneself and one's writing seriously – blunt confession, John – the anguish of the heart. The telling – the revelation – the exposure – of one's deepest fears and desires. But so far – luckily for me – my blunt confessions have always been quite well-disguised. Fortunately – for me – I create such characters and events that no one seems to recognize these creations as – essentially – portraits of me. Or even if they do, all they have is generalities – Miserliness, Helplessness, Kindness, Ghosts of the Present and Ghosts of the Past.

Perhaps he'll know

A boy reading a book in a prison cell.
A group of people speaking with one voice.
A closet filled with choices of clothing.

why I find myself

How many people have you known?
How have you known them?
In how many ways?

in this trackless land.

Whether I shall turn out to be the hero of my own life.
Whether that station will be held by anybody else.
These pages must show.

People write to me all the time, John – they accost me on the street. They want me to talk about my characters – why I write this and why I write that. They want to know what is concealed behind my books. So far, their darts have bounced off my chest, John – their arrows have never penetrated beyond these battered walls. But – and here's the conundrum – here is the fear that keeps me awake. With each new story – with each new setting – with each new character I create – I am getting – I know I am, John – it keeps me awake all through the night – closer and closer to the fires that burn like coals in the very darkest depths of my secret soul.

Nobody knows it better than you.

He walked the length of the town. East to West – North to South. All the people were very busy – life was keeping them occupied. They barely noticed him as he passed them on the street.

He was a posthumous child, his father having died.

"Dickens's characters are a case of humanity caught and made permanent at its highest and most extreme mood."

"A Dickens novel's unifying themes are stated and restated in various keys throughout the entire work."

Dickens telling me that he wants to keep his secrets.
I wonder if he will tell me what they are.

He knew exactly what he wanted.
He wrote it clearly in his will.
He wanted his unfinished book to be published.
Each with a bottle of ink and a quill.

I'd like to ask him - worn a deep groove - plunges into the scene - created for a reason - what dark corners - i have no idea - snuffed his candle out - the action of the sand - toss the smooth stone - my eyes were open.

This lunatic, in letting Scrooge's nephew out, had let two other people in. They were portly gentlemen, pleasant to behold, and now stood, with their hats off, in Scrooge's office. They had books and papers in their hands, and bowed to him.

"Scrooge and Marley's, I believe," said one of the gentlemen, referring to his list. "Have I the pleasure of addressing Mr. Scrooge, or Mr. Marley?"

"Mr. Marley has been dead these seven years," Scrooge replied. "He died seven years ago, this very night."

"We have no doubt his liberality is well represented by his surviving partner," said the gentleman, presenting his credentials.

It certainly was; for they had been two kindred spirits. At the ominous word "liberality," Scrooge

frowned, and shook his head, and handed the credentials back.

"At this festive season of the year, Mr. Scrooge," said the gentleman, taking up a pen, "it is more than usually desirable that we should make some slight provision for the Poor and destitute, who suffer greatly at the present time. Many thousands are in want of common necessaries; hundreds of thousands are in want of common comforts, sir."

"Are there no prisons?" asked Scrooge.

"Plenty of prisons," said the gentleman, laying down the pen again.

"And the Union workhouses?" demanded Scrooge. "Are they still in operation?"

"They are. Still," returned the gentleman, "I wish I could say they were not."

"The Treadmill and the Poor Law are in full vigour, then?" said Scrooge.

"Both very busy, sir."

"Oh! I was afraid, from what you said at first, that something had occurred to stop them in their useful course," said Scrooge. "I'm very glad to hear it."

said the third.

The boy sits on the floor of the cell. The boy is Dickens – it has to be. He tries to read a book and covers his ears. There is the mother, the father and another man as well. All three adults argue above him. I can see, but I cannot hear. The two men gesture and point, in turn, at the boy. Their faces grow red as they gesture. The mother's tears flow down her face. The children cling to her skirts. They are terrified.

No outline would be visible.

Now don't misunderstand me, John – what everyone knows is what I am – every reader can say that he knows of what I am made. It's just that Charles Dickens is a restless throng of beings, John – as is, I assume, every creature on the earth. Well, perhaps not everyone, John – many are pleased with their lot in life – I suspect this to be true, John, about you – but a group of selves inhabits my restless soul. And that is what I am, John – a restless, restless soul. I have everything I dreamed of when I was – well, let us say when I was a boy – and yet I can never sleep a whole night without terrible dreams.

Had seen him grow
as a sprawling weed.

There was blacking on this fingers as he worked.

He would look far beyond
his reflected face.

To begin my life with the beginning of my life.
I record that I was born at twelve o'clock at night.
The clock began to strike – I began to cry.

Writing is peeling away the layers, John. So far, all my secrets have held. Layer after layer of scenes and characters – in a fictional, fictional world. Readers laugh and cry at the wonders that they behold. This book, John – this Christmas-story – will be one more peel of the onion, and the characters, John, are warning me – not just the ones that you have seen – that I am the one who is suffering – living and dying each day and each moment – deep at the core. I have always stood in the shadows, John, but my characters are warning me – that I am edging – with this tale, John – this simple Christmas-tale – ever closer – ever closer to the light.

An unprofitable dream.

Scars would break out on his heart. Scars would break out on his mind. Scars would break out on his sensibility, but not a scar would appear on his hands or on his face.

The man promptly turned him upside down.

"In a Dickens novel, a character is confronted, either with his double or with his opposite."

"The character is invited to see his defects as enlarged, isolated, unmistakably his own – detached for inspection."

Seeing Dickens with his parents when he was a boy.
Puzzling out just how this imagery applies to me.

All the clues would be well-hidden.
Doppelgangers by the score.
Red-herrings strewn on the pathways.
Cul-de-sacs on a moonless night.

A multiplicity of simplistic elements - currents of the air - far away from anything - a challenging read - one's deepest fears and desires - reveal a concern - set like stone - a bag of seeds - the clean, white snow - change the whole house.

"Under the impression that they scarcely furnish Christian cheer of mind or body to the multitude," returned the gentleman, "a few of us are endeavouring to raise a fund to buy the Poor some meat and drink, and means of warmth. We choose this time, because it is a time, of all others, when Want is keenly felt, and Abundance rejoices. What shall I put you down for?"

"Nothing!" Scrooge replied.

"You wish to be anonymous?"

"I wish to be left alone," said Scrooge. "Since you ask me what I wish, gentlemen, that is my answer. I don't make merry myself at Christmas and I can't afford to make idle people merry. I help to support the establishments I have mentioned – they cost enough; and those who are badly off must go there."

"Many can't go there; and many would rather die."

"If they would rather die," said Scrooge, "they had better do it, and decrease the surplus population. Besides – excuse me – I don't know that."

"But you might know it," observed the gentleman.

"It's not my business," Scrooge returned. "It's enough for a man to understand his own business, and not to interfere with other people's. Mine occupies me constantly. Good afternoon, gentlemen!"

Seeing clearly that it would be useless to pursue their point, the gentlemen withdrew. Scrooge resumed his labours with an improved opinion of himself, and in a more facetious temper than was usual with him.

He hoped –
one day –
to get to know
himself.

Is Dickens showing me these scenes or am I creating them on my own? He obviously doesn't realize that I've read about him in all the books. All the biographies tell of these scenes and explain what they mean. So – am I seeing them without his knowledge? Does Dickens think that he's keeping his childhood a secret from me? Or – is he showing all this to me, but leaving me alone – to puzzle out the significance on my own? If so – then what's the purpose? What does this have to do with the scenes where he acts as my guide?

The father slumps on the bench. I can't tell who the other man is. He pokes the boy with his toe. The boy looks up from the book. The mother reaches out her hand and lets it fall. The man gestures toward the door. The boy looks at the mother – the mother looks at the father – the father slumps on the bench and stares at the wall. The boy closes the book and places it on the floor.

The boy gets up and follows the man, who walks to the door. The children huddle with the mother as she cries.

To know its value.

Would you say that there is a secret to writing, Mr. Dickens? Or would you simply say that it's talent plus technique? That you are simply born with powers of observation, and that this insight gives you something worthwhile to say?

These are obviously scenes from his life. But – I can't figure out why he doesn't plunge into these scenes and pull me after him. Why am I watching them all alone? Why am I not invited inside? It's the perfect opportunity to tell me what he thinks – and how he feels. Childhood trauma – searing experiences – 'the child is father of the man'. I don't get the feeling that he knows that I already know.

He could see, on the distant horizon, a faint line of shore.

Perhaps the beautiful tropical island of his dreams.

The journey led

An author rehearsing his characters before he writes.
A person showing another how to dance.
A man who answers to two names.

through bogs and briars –

Do you turn people into mythical creatures?
Does it help you to know them better?
Or does it mean that you know them even less?

the tangled landscape of story-land.

And what was Dickens's father's childhood, by the way? Did it make him what he was? Shouldn't I be seeing more than I already know? These are scenes that I've known all my life. I read about Dickens's childhood in my twenties, when I was reading the novels, and wanted to connect the novels with Dickens's life. But no one seems to write about Dickens's father – at least not the father's childhood, before Dickens came along. So why – in these visions – don't I get to see the father's childhood now? Why am I given a re-hash of all these familiar scenes?

Looked here and there to find himself.

The scars would fester in the night, as he tossed and turned on his bed. Then he would rise up in the morning and start the walk of agony again.

Chapter 6

Look here! – John – look here!, Dickens is saying. This is old Scrooge – who starts the story! He is the character who will be in every stave! Five staves should allow me to do it – I always plan my tales. I am going to explain to Scrooge how I want him to be. See him standing in his bedroom! – in his nightgown and tasseled cap! He is mild mannered, John – as he will be when the end of the tale is told. But I plan to make him a curmudgeon – stingy and selfish and bitter and cruel. It's for contrast, John – for contrast. I shall explain this to him today. Come along with me, John, as I talk to him! I will give him an acting lesson – which he badly needs! Dickens plunges into the scene and I find myself mysteriously drawn in too.

Thrown into greatest alarm.

So – tell me, John, are you a writer? Oh, excuse me – of course you are. I should have asked – do you *feel* yourself to be? Consult the memory that I have given you. Have you written – scribbled – scrawled – a book or two? Do you write novels, such as do I? – well no one writes like me. Do you write novels such as Thackeray, or perhaps Collins, tends to do? What is your modus operandi? – what is a novel, John, to you? Does it tell, perhaps, your secrets? Or does it – ostensibly, at least – have absolutely nothing to do with you? You have the ills of your society – even Canada must have a few ills. Are your characters social-beings or are they you? What dark corners does the lantern-light reveal?

Perhaps he'll know

A clock that cannot be seen through the fog.
A character who is creating another character.
A mystery story which has no clues.

a path that leads

What is your favourite Dickens story?
Does it illuminate your life?
Does any particular story embody your hopes and your fears?

through these endless grains of sand.

Michaelmas term lately over.
The Lord Chancellor sitting in Lincoln's Inn Hall.
Implacable November weather.

There was a cave on the side of a mountain. The entrance was hidden behind a huge rock. He stumbled on it as he searched for a lamb from his fold.
To no purpose.
I'm starting to see you, John, as a writer of interesting books – in the novel that I'm thinking of writing about you. The whole story about you – yes, you and your deepest concerns – is gradually taking shape – producing a form – a tale – a narrative – in the depths of my mind. You will have – I see it forming – something very dark in your past. What it is I do not now know, but

it will come to me as I brood. Something you'll keep – concealed from everyone – in the deepest, darkest recesses of your mind. You shall form – in your mind – a story – a story which, as a writer in my story, you will write. Your novel – your fictional novel – will be at the core of a novel of mine. And you – as a writer – a fictional-writer, John – a writer created by me – will write a novel – will imagine and write a novel, in your turn. And you will figure out a problem – a problem with which you wrestle, John, in the very depths of your soul – a problem that threatens every ink-stained wretch in the writing trade.

There were giants whispering secrets as he was born.

"Dickens is, by far, his own best critic."
"Dickens has written that by the intensity of his imagination he is able to perceive relations in things which are not generally apparent."

I have fallen overboard! I can't breathe! I am plunging down, down to the ocean floor!

So Dickens is making me into a writer.
Perhaps I should tell him that I've already performed that task.

I can breathe! I can breathe! Fortunately, the earth is a sphere! I am bobbing on the surface of the other side!

Groping and floundering condition - depths of the ocean - will create together - experiences the point of view - too short to cover them - stares at the open door -

*back against the wall - nothing cold-blooded - love the
sun - carry the empty boxes.*

Meanwhile the fog and darkness thickened so, that
people ran about with flaring links, proffering their ser-
vices to go before horses in carriages, and conduct them
on their way. The ancient tower of a church, whose gruff
old bell was always peeping slyly down at Scrooge out
of a Gothic window in the wall, became invisible, and
struck the hours and quarters in the clouds, with tremu-
lous vibrations afterwards as if its teeth were chattering
in its frozen head up there.

The cold became intense. In the main street, at the
corner of the court, some labourers were repairing the
gas-pipes, and had lighted a great fire in a brazier, round
which a party of ragged men and boys were gathered:
warming their hands and winking their eyes before the
blaze in rapture. The water-plug being left in solitude,
its overflowings sullenly congealed, and turned to mis-
anthropic ice.

*He was born
on the dark side
of the moon.*

Old scrooge is in his nightcap – I recognize the
scene. He doesn't seem to notice me as Dickens ef-
fusively explains. The scene is entirely silent for me.
Luckily Dickens is an excellent mime – I can see everything he wants old Scrooge to do – and to be. Dickens dives beneath the covers – he makes himself small
and frail and afraid. But, abruptly, he throws off the
covers and leaps to the floor again. He seizes the old

fellow's nightcap – pulls it down over his own head – and then he dives back into the bed again. Now Dickens lies there in his nightcap – just his head is visible now. His eyes pop out in fear – he says a few words to the watching Scrooge – but I cannot hear a word that Dickens says. Dickens shivers in absolute horror – he croaks feebly to an imaginary ghost – every word of response is a painful dart in his ear. Every once in a while, he turns and explains the scene. Scrooge stands beside me and takes it all in – the two of us just stand and watch Dickens emote. Just an ordinary old man – not the gruff Scrooge from the Christmas-story at all. It is Dickens who is Scrooge as I watch the scene. I feel the cold as Dickens mimes it – my teeth are chattering and my blood is like ice. I wonder if Old Scrooge – the non-Dickens Scrooge – feels the same. Dickens throws off the covers and jumps back out – still in his shoes – and snatches the nightcap from his head and tosses it back to Scrooge again. Scrooge misses it and it falls down on the floor. Dickens puts his arm around Scrooge and points to the spot where he saw the ghost. He pops his eyes and points at Scrooge's eyes and leans in close to Scrooge's face and looks deep into his mind, as if he were placing the other Scrooge – the Scrooge-who-will-be-Scrooge – under a spell. Scrooge is trying to look down at his nightcap – he is thinking of something else. He listens as if he's a schoolboy learning by rote.

They had been strangers.

How to write of your deepest experiences, John – of your deepest, darkest concerns – with not one of your readers ever suspecting the truth. You will be telling your story, John – yes, telling your story and all it entails – but a story that not one reader will come to know. You'll be surrounded by your characters, John – short and thin and fat and tall – and not a one will have your nose or your mouth or your eyes. Yes, your story will be about you, John – however, your story will *seem* to be about everyone but yourself. Not one reader who turns the page will pick up on one clue.

Had seen him raise his face to the sky
and drink the rain.

The boy grew up to be a famous author.

Deep into the furrows
of his brain.

Much mud in the streets.
The waters newly retired from the face of the earth.
A megalosaurus waddling up Holborn Hill.

This is the entrance to the underworld. Here the souls of the dead do dwell. When I meet them, they will tell me what they've learned.
The very heart of the fog.
Oh I am so glad that I have created you, John. You are one of the most interesting characters I have ever conceived. So far from me – your creator – Charles Dickens – in every particular. You are a truly imaginative creation – the placing of myself in a realm that is entirely outré – a character whose story will seem to have nothing to do with me. It was – for sure – my visit to Canada – a world and an ocean of thought away. It opened, for my imagination, an entirely new field of exploration. It will be my greatest novel, John, and you will play your part. Yes – the story of a writer – a colonial – a Canadian – which – on the surface, John,

at least – will have absolutely nothing to do with me.

The man threatened to tear his heart and liver out.

"No novelist has profited more richly than Dickens from not examining what goes on in his own mind."
"Dickens is not able and not willing to analyze the relations between the inner-being of his characters and their outer-selves."

I am crawling on the floor of a jungle! Tedious minute by tedious minute by tedious minute! I dislodge each tedious minute with my nose!

Seeing the original Scrooge in person, as if I were meeting him on the street.
Trying not to be disappointed at what I see.

I am crawling on the floor of a jungle! My rescue ship is waiting in the harbour! I can smell the salt of the seashore with my nose!

A multiplicity of simplistic elements - currents of the air - far away from anything - a challenging read - one's deepest fears and desires - reveal a concern - set like stone - a bag of seeds - the clean, white snow - change the whole house.

The brightness of the shops where holly sprigs and berries crackled in the lamp heat of the windows, made pale faces ruddy as they passed. Poulterers' and grocers' trades became a splendid joke: a glorious pageant, with which it was next to impossible to believe that such dull principles as bargain and sale had anything to do.

The Lord Mayor, in the stronghold of the mighty Mansion House, gave orders to his fifty cooks and butlers to keep Christmas as a Lord Mayor's household should; and even the little tailor, whom he had fined five shillings on the previous Monday for being drunk and bloodthirsty in the streets, stirred up to-morrow's pudding in his garret, while his lean wife and the baby sallied out to buy the beef.

It comes to us as glass,
said the mirror-maker.

I can't believe that this is happening. This Scrooge is not the Scrooge of the Christmas-story – the person beside me is an entirely different man. I turn to talk to him, but he sits down on the bed and starts to cry. Dickens sits on the bed beside him. He puts his arm around Scrooge and he speaks – in what I take to be soothing words. Scrooge raises his tear-filled eyes and looks off in the distance. I wonder if the distance happens to be me. I am directly in his line of sight, but I can't tell, through the tears, whether he even knows that I am in the room. The two of them – author and character – make a very disturbing sight. Scrooge wipes the tears from his cheeks – Dickens offers his handkerchief. Scrooge shakes his head and softly cries some more. I can't believe that this is happening. What a sentimental old man – I have no idea what has set him off in this way. Does Dickens want me to speak to him? He said he would want my help – that I was being created to soothe his characters – to intercede and ease a divide. I expect him to call upon me – this seems an appropriate time. I open my mouth to speak, but I find no words. It seems that I am a mime character too.

Something strange to me.

How much of yourself is in your characters, Mr. Dickens? How much of yourself do you keep in reserve? If you would speak in percentages, it would help to explain what is probably a very complex idea.

Scrooge, in person, is not very animated at all. Even his tears are gentle rain-drops – I would have expected – from him – a raging typhoon. He's certainly not an actor, that's for sure. It's hard to tell whether Scrooge – the still-unwritten Scrooge – understands what it is that Dickens will want him to do – when he comes back to Scrooge's bedroom and writes the scene in which Scrooge is going to play his part. I wonder if Dickens is disappointed that Scrooge is not a very good actor. Does he see Scrooge as not quite adequate for the role? Can Dickens replace him? – is that an option? Or does he see something inside of Scrooge – an essence – an inner-quality – of which Scrooge – the actual Scrooge – is not aware – that will be evident to Scrooge when he and Dickens – holding hands at the edge of a cliff – make a leap and plunge down deeper than he has ever – in his life as the Dickens-less Scrooge – descended before?

He plunged into the water and swam towards the shore.

He swam with half the strength that he felt remained.

It led through all

One person explaining something to another.

Themes that are stated in various keys.
A reader experiencing a point of view.

the styles and genres,

Who is your favourite Dickens character?
Is there one who is just like you?
Have you been captured and exhibited in a Dickens tale?

techniques and modes.

He went down in search of wisdom. His sheep were left in the fold. The lost lamb was bleating in the field.
The blood had stopped forever.
What is it that Dickens wants me to see? Why has he invited me to watch these rehearsals – if that's what he considers these visits to be – to watch him present his ideas to the characters – show them how he wants them to act – wants them to be? Does he know that I'm seeing the disagreements – the contentions – the differences of opinion? The reluctance – the recalcitrance – the unwillingness to take part? Who or what is controlling these visions? And what are these visions supposed to mean to me?

Chapter 7

Of course – it's the Marshalsea prison. A cave-like cell with bars on the door. But the door isn't locked – it is sitting ajar. The man, the woman, the children – the same family as before. It's the family of Charles Dickens – what else could it possibly be? Dickens's family in debtor's prison – the Marshalsea. The children play with their toys on the bare stone floor. Dickens's mother shivers and clutches her tattered shawl. Dickens's father sits on the bench and flinches as he stares at the open door. Perhaps he hears footsteps, but I hear nothing – all is mime where I am concerned. The boy – Charles Dickens – must be approaching. The Marshalsea is now the Dickens family home.

Conversations apparently so trivial.

What in the world is Dickens up to? I just can't figure it out. He keeps insisting that he has created me. But if he did, then why do I keep believing that I'm real? Our realities are at odds – if he believes what he says he believes. And if he doesn't – then what reason could he possibly have to pretend?

Perhaps he'll know

A family in a prison with an open door.
A force which limits communication.

The wedding of a princess and a prince.

all the things

How do you choose a topic of interest?
Does each topic reveal a concern?
What is the point of exploring a topic by way of a book?

I'd like to know.

Now what I want is facts.
Nothing but facts.
Facts alone are wanted.

I could blow this whole thing sky-high. I could say that I already knew – Mr. Dickens – that you visited Canada. I read about it in the books that were written about you after you died. I was born a hundred years after you visited Niagara Falls. And what's all this blather about this book that you plan to write? I'm not your character – not a fiction – not a figment of one of your dreams! I'm a human – I'm flesh and blood – as real as you! But – I know I'm not going to do that. It would be impolite – aggressive – confrontational. It would bounce the whole thing into a completely different sphere.

A loophole in the thick stone wall.

A gigantic megalosaurus waddled along the street. He had been asleep in a bog for he didn't know how many years. He was looking for a herd of megalosauridae. They had wandered off in search of food and left him behind.

His mother was an ineffectual being, who expected to die while giving birth.

"Dickens uses the materials of the popular literature and culture of his childhood such as pantomime and romance."
"He brings the weight of mature awareness to the old forms of the folk-tale and the fairy-tale."

Wondering whether I should wrest control of this strange journey.
Afraid I might crash if I don't follow Dickens's light in the fog.

He knew exactly what he wanted.
He wrote it clearly in his will.
He wanted his unfinished book to be published.
Each with a bottle of ink and a quill.

Making up the complexity - answered to both names - seemingly lost all coherence - quite dark already - they want to know - the entrance was hidden - make the best bargain - ever solved the mystery - and ease a divide - to get to talk.

Foggier yet, and colder. Piercing, searching, biting cold. If the good Saint Dunstan had but nipped the Evil Spirit's nose with a touch of such weather as that, instead of using his familiar weapons, then indeed he would have roared to lusty purpose.

The owner of one scant young nose, gnawed and mumbled by the hungry cold as bones are gnawed by dogs, stooped down at Scrooge's keyhole to regale him with a Christmas carol: but at the first sound of

"God bless you, merry gentleman!
May nothing you dismay!"

Scrooge seized the ruler with such energy of action, that the singer fled in terror, leaving the keyhole to the fog and even more congenial frost.

*He always thought
he'd like to travel.*

Dickens's father sits and stares at the boy – the boy-Dickens – as he stands at the door of the cell. The mother looks from father to son and back again. The children huddle under a blanket in a corner of the room. The boy – the boy-Dickens – holds out his hand and stands and waits. What age would he be, I wonder? – he was always small in stature – ten or twelve? – or perhaps thirteen? I've read about all this – many times in many biographies over the years. The boy's fist is clenched. He holds it out towards his father. The father stares at the boy. The son – Charles Dickens – stands at the door of the cell and thrusts his fist towards his father with something inside. Oh – the book? I look for the book – I look for the book that the boy was reading. I look, but the book is nowhere to be seen.

Connected with a thousand thoughts.

And yet – I have to wonder why I'm so placidly playing along. I wonder why I'm letting him get away with this. We're like two people – two knockabouts – Dickens and I – two vagabonds – and one is telling a story – gathering a crowd as he spins a yarn – and the other one is startled at all the – inaccuracies – embellishments – inventions – fabrications – in the story that his companion is telling – relating – composing – inventing – conceiving and bringing to birth. A juggler convincing the crowd that he's juggling nuggets of gold from exotic lands while what he's spinning is a blur of local stones that he picked up and painted, the day before, along the road. But the second fellow – the comic side-kick – the dull assistant – the thick-headed friend – he doesn't say anything at all. If a nugget should happen to fall, he would snatch it up and keep it concealed and hand it back to resume its place in the whirling blur. He stands in the glow of the brilliant dazzle and doesn't interrupt or deny. Because he's a listener too – the story is about his travels – he stands there wondering where the story is going to go.

*And he knew
all the houses.*

He wrote books that made the people laugh and cry.

*There he saw the many denizens
of a crowded room.*

*Plant nothing else.
Root out everything else.
Stick to the facts.*

It's quite amazing, though, to imagine – it's quite an intriguing thought – to imagine what being a character in a Dickens novel would be like. This would put me in the company of Mr. Pickwick and Oliver and Sairey Gamp – and even of people – of characters – that Dickens – this Dickens, anyway – has not yet even imagined

– like – Sydney Carton – and – Edwin Drood. Though – I don't know – I still can't see myself as an author – even a fictional author in a novel – of the Dickens stamp.

He dreaded that he saw new meaning.

He reached the tallest building. He stopped waddling and stood still. He bent down his head and looked at a window, but all he could see was one gigantic eye.

The hands of dead people reached up out of graves.

"A Dickens character is intent on creating an identity in a world of dizzying circumstances."

"A Dickens character is as much a creative artist as Dickens himself, as the Dickens character must create an imaginary person in order to define and celebrate the self."

Watching the boy-Dickens and his family in debtor's prison.

Intriguing thoughts about what a novelist would make of me.

Perhaps the author would be the victim.
Perhaps the author would wield the knife.
Perhaps the author would be the detective.
Perhaps the author would not be involved.

Brings me back to the point - solitary as an oyster - an alternative grid - not been light all day - the fear that keeps me awake - concealed from everyone - the cassandra in the story - bring a smooth stone home - imagine them to be - no eye at all.

At length the hour of shutting up the counting-house arrived. With an ill-will Scrooge dismounted from his stool, and tacitly admitted the fact to the expectant clerk in the Tank, who instantly snuffed his candle out, and put on his hat.

"You'll want all day to-morrow, I suppose?" said Scrooge.

"If quite convenient, sir."

"It's not convenient," said Scrooge, "and it's not fair. If I was to stop half-a-crown for it, you'd think yourself ill-used, I'll be bound?"

The clerk smiled faintly.

"And yet," said Scrooge, "you don't think me ill-used, when I pay a day's wages for no work."

We put a coat of silvering
on the back.

Story-tellers tell stories. That's what they do. They are alchemists with words. They pluck gold-dust out of the air and melt a handful down and pour the liquid into a mold of their own devising – a mold of their own shape and size. A boy in a blacking warehouse becomes a boy in an orphanage – with a bowl in his hands – wanting more. So – what does a Canadian, from a wood-lot near Niagara Falls, become, when he is plucked, by a master story-teller, out of the air?

The prison cell again. Early sunlight streaming through the window-bars. The boy is dipping his hands in the basin. He splashes water over his face. He dries his face on the arm of his sleeve. The father sits on the bench and stares. The mother draws the blanket closer.

She has her back against the wall. The children's heads peep out of the blanket as they sleep. The boy – Dickens, the boy – it must be him, though I have no guide – doesn't look at his father. The father stares straight ahead. The boy's face is set like stone. He doesn't look around. He walks across the cell towards the door.

Unaltered in his outward form.

I never hear your characters talk, Mr. Dickens. I see you talking to them and see them talking to you, but I never hear what either of you has to say. I hear you when we are alone – presumably, you hear me. This is very strange to me. It is very strange, indeed. Is it strange to you?

Actually, he's quite the forceful author. In the process of making me a character – a Dickens character – a Dickens author-character – he'll no doubt take me by the shoulders and set me aside and show me – in mime, of course, but with a mixture of mime and words – the character that he's decided I'm going to be. Perhaps he'll write me – write my novel – and my novel-within-a-novel – after he writes *A Christmas Carol*, which – wait a minute! Which he wrote in – 1843!

He stopped swimming and felt with his toes for a ledge on which to walk.

When he failed, he turned and swam to the rock again.

Through all the literary eras

A shepherd seeking wisdom at the entrance to the underworld.
Two people whose eyes are fused together.

A book with an un-printed ending.

of ancient

Do books make life seem simpler?
Do they make it seem more complex?
What service, exactly, does a book provide?

and modern times.

Slow down here – let me think – let me think a little bit. Surely this isn't going to happen – this cannot come to be. A Dickens-Passfield novel would not be historical – is not historical. There is – can't be – can be – no such thing. But of course, Dickens can't possibly know this. He's alive and clearing his path as he moves through time. Hacking his path, it seems to me. He's not a creature out-of-time, as, presumably, am I. Should I tell him? – tell him everything? – or just wait and see where all of this mystery-novel talk is going to lead?

A short period of blank astonishment.

A crowd had gathered to watch the megalosaurus. He's looking for his mother, said the little boy's mother. He's looking for his father, said the little boy's father. He just wants to see himself, said the little boy.

Chapter 8

Look here, John!, Dickens is saying. Come closer and have a look! A mother and her children – young Peter, the girl, Martha, and the two younger Cratchits. 'Cratchit' – you see – is going to be the family name. They are huddled around the fireplace – in search of a little warmth. See – a watery soup is all they will have to eat. The father will be a clerk in Scrooge's office – he will scratch out a living with his pen. Now where is he? – oh here he is – with his boy upon his shoulder – come in at the door. See how the children all crowd around as the two of them enter the room? A loving family, John – a loving family to be sure. And look at the crutch – and the iron frame on the little limbs. 'Tiny Tim' will be the name of the boy who is lame. But come on, John! – let's get busy! Come along with me while I visit the Cratchit home!

The lantern that has no light in it.

Why can you not hear the characters speaking? Well, that's a very good question, John. Now, I suppose, there is some force – some character or person – some entity, shall we say – that has the power of control, and who also has a purpose – a plan – a logic – about what you are able to hear and what you cannot. But you can hear every word I say – when I am talking to you directly. That is the case – in this exchange – is it not? So

– ask me anything that you would care to know.

Perhaps he'll be

A force which limits perception.
A person who disappears from the scene.
A book that has not yet been written.

a writer

Is Dickens answering any of your questions?
Is he giving you a chance to ask?
Would you say that you are reluctant to pin him down?

like I am.

My father's family name.
My infant tongue could make of both names.
Nothing longer or more explicit.

I will not look over my shoulder. I will not turn – I will not look back. It's a lesson I have learned from fairy-tales.
No one knows for certain.
The Christmas-characters can't hear you either, John, but they are very aware of you, John, all the same. They have become more and more aware of you as a presence of some sort as time has gone on. They haven't accepted you yet. They're what you might call a clannish group – not easily approached – quick to start. In fact, John, they are rather leery of you. They have been asking me why you are here and what you stand for. But you can dismiss these concerns from your mind. They

haven't yet warmed up to you – seen you as one of their fellow-characters – seen the story in which I shall place you – seen how close you are to my heart – seen you as one of the group that clusters around me in my chair in my writing room – to bolster me – nourish me – protect me – as I work.

His aunt intended to guide him if he were a girl.

"A Dickens novel shows us that life is not a straight path, but a series of crossroads."
"A Dickens novel presents an imagined metaphorical world which stands as a model by which to explore the realities of actual life."

Boiled cabbage once again! In the workhouse of my thought! The thin gruel of penance in a bowl!

Probing Dickens about what he knows about what's going on.
Trying to assess just how candid he is willing to be.

Boiled cabbage in the workhouse! The smell of penance in the air! I hold out my bowl and ask for more!

Not perfectly convinced - imagine a story for you - an integrated pattern - were mere phantoms - barely notice him - a problem that threatens - exploring a topic - stares at the open door - very strange to me - an unrelenting demand.

The clerk observed that it was only once a year.
"A poor excuse for picking a man's pocket every twenty-fifth of December!" said Scrooge, buttoning his

great-coat to the chin. "But I suppose you must have the whole day. Be here all the earlier next morning."

The clerk promised that he would; and Scrooge walked out with a growl.

The office was closed in a twinkling, and the clerk, with the long ends of his white comforter dangling below his waist (for he boasted no great-coat), went down a slide on Cornhill, at the end of a lane of boys, twenty times, in honour of its being Christmas Eve, and then ran home to Camden Town as hard as he could pelt, to play at blindman's-buff.

Go and live
somewhere else.

Dickens takes the Cratchits by surprise. I land on both feet on the edge of this family scene. The children back away, as Dickens launches into a speech. I hear no words, but I read them on his face. He is lying on the bare table, miming the succulence of the turkey. He sighs as he basks in the swelling heat of the oven – he smiles as he savours his own nose-tickling juices – he cringes as he awaits the first cut of the knife. Then he leaps back down to the floor and accosts the Cratchits, one by one. He takes Mrs. Cratchit by the shoulders and moves her in front of the table. Then he moves Bob Cratchit aside. Dickens takes a jug from the hearth – in mime, there is no jug – and he almost burns his fingers, so he seizes a protective rag – a comforter which he strips from a startled Bob Cratchit – and winds it around his hand as he lifts the imaginary jug and pours an imaginary drink into an imaginary glass. A spilled drop singes his forearm and he flinches, momentarily, but he shrugs it off and pours a second glass – all without there being a single glass in the room. Then he mimes – he mimes as Bob – the picking up of a glass and the giving of a tender speech – wordless for me, of course – but his eyes – the Dickens-Cratchit eyes – are glowing brightly and the Dickens-Cratchit lips form a forgiving and resigned, yet kindly, smile. Then he pauses – while raising the glass – the imaginary glass – and takes Bob Cratchit by the shoulders and moves him into place, and then moves Mrs. Cratchit aside and mimes her part. Again a mimed glass – he placed the first one and the comforter on the table a moment ago – but this time, a troubled face – a Mrs-Cratchit-Dickens face – a face with strong emotion and anguished thought. Love for her husband – anger at life – resignation dragging her down – a few bitter words that I can't hear and finally she takes a sip from the glass – a Mrs-Cratchit-Dickens sip – that curdles her haggard features, and all the wretchedness of her life is there to see. The two Cratchits stare at Dickens as he plays their parts. I stand and admire the performance – no one seems to notice me. Dickens cannot resist a bow to end the scene. The two Cratchits do not respond – not with anything like glee – to Dickens's antics. Their minds are on something other than this cheerful – or is it tearful? – Christmas scene.

The evidence of my own senses.

They have come to wonder, John, whether – perhaps – you just might know too much about my life – my background – my youth – for my own good. That I might have told you my secrets – my early – difficulties – setbacks – traumas, if you will. But that, you'll say, is ridiculous, as you know – and I know, too – that over the course of these visits, I have told you nothing of myself – nothing pertinent or significant at all.

He said he was counting on me to help him. He said he was open for advice. He said he would call on me to calm the waters – to interject – intervene – intercede. And yet he has been completely silent – he's never once mentioned that role, again, for me. Why would he tell me of his plans and then not proceed?

Knew all the alleys
and cul-de-sacs.

People gathered on the street in front of the window.

He would pick the one
that appealed to him that day.

On the authority of his tombstone.
I never saw any likeness of either of them.
My first fancies regarding what they were.

If I do, I'll turn to stone. I'll turn into a pillar of salt. If I do, I'll have to return to the underworld.
No sense of sequence.
All human interaction is barter, John – what one has and what one needs. You might have matches – you might have firewood – you look for someone who has what you lack. With some people, you share an agenda – with others, your agendas are at odds. You make bargains in the marketplace – the marketplace of the heart – there is nothing cold-blooded in any of this at all. You take home, from the market, a turkey for a feast – you take home a bag of seeds which you hope will

grow. You make the best bargain that you can make on a given day. If it rains, you'll be soaking wet when you arrive home.

A beacon and a gibbet stood nearby.

"The truths of a Dickens novel cannot be appreciated from the outside."
"The reader must participate in a Dickens novel in order to appreciate that there is any truth at all."

The cobblestones on the street are my hopes and my dreams! I cannot avoid soiling them as I walk! I need to walk the streets to get to my home!

I have never seen the Cratchits so serious and so disturbed.
I wonder if Dickens knows the Cratchits any better than do I.

I am stuck on this corner of the street! I wait as the street-sweeper toils! He is attempting to sweep the mire from the cobblestones!

The same water - telling me who i am - attempting to imagine - a part of the promised tour - a case of humanity - giants whispering secrets - reveal a concern - set me aside - a moment's irresolution - the legend had said.

Scrooge took his melancholy dinner in his usual melancholy tavern; and having read all the newspapers, and beguiled the rest of the evening with his banker's-book, went home to bed.

He lived in chambers which had once belonged to his deceased partner. They were a gloomy suite of rooms, in a lowering pile of building up a yard, where it had so little business to be, that one could scarcely help fancying it must have run there when it was a young house, playing at hide-and-seek with other houses, and forgotten the way out again.

> *People looking at the glass*
> *call it a mirror,*

Oh – why am I so suspicious? Why do I think that Dickens has something to hide? Sure – his childhood, but other than that, I don't see any reason for him – for his characters – to feel uneasy about me. I'm the one who's keeping secrets. I know more about him than he could possibly know about me. I'm Cassandra, that's what I am. I'm the Cassandra in the story of Dickens's life. I know everything that's going to happen to him – how long he'll live – what books he'll write. He doesn't have any secrets from me. Except about Ellen Ternan – and – Edwin Drood. But what is it that Dickens thinks he knows about me?

It's not exactly an argument. As before, I don't hear a word. The two Cratchits sit down at the table, with Mrs. Cratchit adjusting Bob's comforter as he shrugs it on. Dickens implores them – I watch in mime. The two Cratchits shake their heads – the Christmas-characters refuse to budge. The children look from their parents to Dickens and back again. Dickens mimes Bob Cratchit carving. He sharpens the knife at an imaginary grind-stone and sticks the plump, well-basted turkey with the fork. Slowly he carves the slices of turkey – his face is ecstatic at the smell. The succulence makes me hungry – I feel a knife and fork in my hands. Then he mimes scooping the potatoes – hot and steaming – from the bowl. A flagon of gravy – a treat to the eyes and the nose and the mouth. All in mime, as there is no gravy on the table – nor anywhere else in the room. My mouth is watering as he speaks, but I hear no words. The young Cratchits' eyes grow wide – they are hungry – they are starving – they hope against hope that their parents will yield. The Cratchit parents refuse the offer and shake their heads. They have a resistance that Dickens – who made them – cannot believe.

Gave this first proof.

Would you say, Mr. Dickens, that the topic is never the topic? That a reader can misunderstand what an author means? That a reading of one of your books – of any book, for that matter – is highly personal? That we make, in the act of reading, a book of our own?

Dickens's plan – his thought – his conception – is very intriguing. Who wouldn't want to be a character in a book? The early Dickens-characters stroll in sunshine – the later ones walk uneasily in the shade. I assume I'll get to negotiate, as the Christmas-characters seem to do. I'll have to ask him for a little more detail.

It was a rock, not an island, so there was nothing to eat or to drink.

All he had were some provisions from the wreck.

It was a search

A story with nothing but facts.

A man stirring a pudding in a garret.
A tour without a guide.

for the perfect fusion

What are the questions that should be asked?
Should you be the one to ask such questions?
Or should Dickens be asking questions of you?

of meaning and form.

But I have an excellent memory. My eyes were open as I walked. I don't need to turn my head when I feel the urge to look back as I trudge along the trail from the underworld.

A galvanizing apparatus.

Will I be arguing with Dickens – or sulking – or bursting into tears – when he comes to show me how he wants me to play my part – in the novel in which he intends to – illuminate – my life? Or will I acquiesce and let him have his way? What if I don't like the role that Dickens assigns to me?

Chapter 9

I know exactly where I am. It's the blacking factory in London. I've read about it many, many times.
I'm standing in front of the window – out on the street.
Who – or what – has brought me here? I know exactly
who this is – this boy who sits on a bench and pastes
the labels onto the bottles in view of the street. Charles
Dickens – Dickens the boy. His eyes look up – into
mine. I know who you are, Charles – I know how you
feel. Please don't look at me this way. I didn't ask to
add to your misery. I did not come to this place of my
own accord.

He saw no likeness of himself.

Well, here's another amazing scene. Not quite deja-vu. Dickens again, in his chair – surrounded by his
characters – but this time, the Christmas-Carol characters are present too. Scrooge – the Fezziwigs – the
Cratchits – the three Ghosts – all mingling with the
Dickens-characters who were here before. The Christmas-Carol characters look more like themselves – at
least, more like I have always imagined them to be –
than they did when I was watching them in rehearsal.
There is relief on some of the faces – the air of suspicion
seems less foreboding. Dickens has, undoubtedly, inter-
ceded – on my behalf – in an effort to dispel the pervad-
ing gloom. Tensions seem to be lessening – smiles lurk

faintly on face after face – conviviality seems about to arrive at the door. But – I'm still standing at a distance from my new-made fellows. I wonder if I can speak to them this time – speak to all the characters, who know, as their faces are saying, that they no longer need be leery – that I am now included in that special Dickens-circle – that I am now a Dickens-character too.

If so

A man looking at a boy through a window.
The making of a bargain in the marketplace.
Torches leading the way through the dark.

he'll speak in imagery

You became a life-long reader in your twenties?
You have been a reader for almost sixty years?
You have studied books and authors all that time?

or in prose.

These times of ours.
No need to be precise.
A boat of dirty and disreputable appearance.

Well, the log-jam has been broken, John. The impasse is no longer there. The characters and I have reached an agreement, John – patched up our differences – made something of a deal – reached an accord. I shall start to write their story as soon as one little, tiny pebble – tiny, but important – is removed from our path.
As good a friend, as good a master, as good a man.
One day the river began to flow upstream. A lad

who was fishing called out to his mother. All of a sudden he noticed the change on his fishing line. All the people in the village ran down to see.

Perhaps the boy would grow up to be an author.

"In reading a Dickens novel, we feel the presence of the novelist – of his disciplined, magisterial sensibility."
"Dickens the narrator acts as a kind of deity, creating and controlling the experience that he imposes upon his readers."

Back in the room with Dickens and his characters.
The cast has changed while I have been watching the fictional scenes.

He knew exactly what he wanted.
He wrote it clearly in his will.
He wanted his unfinished book to be published.
Each with a bottle of ink and a quill.

Clutching the jagged stone - origin of the idea - used to be someone else - nowhere he could turn - stated and restated - bobbing on the surface - exploring a topic - look at the crutch - look cautiously behind - a pair of human eyes.

It was old enough now, and dreary enough, for nobody lived in it but Scrooge, the other rooms being all let out as offices. The yard was so dark that even Scrooge, who knew its every stone, was fain to grope with his hands. The fog and frost so hung about the black old gateway of the house, that it seemed as if the

Genius of the Weather sat in mournful meditation on the threshold.

Now, it is a fact, that there was nothing at all particular about the knocker on the door, except that it was very large. It is also a fact, that Scrooge had seen it, night and morning, during his whole residence in that place; also that Scrooge had as little of what is called fancy about him as any man in the city of London, even including – which is a bold word – the corporation, aldermen, and livery.

But he didn't know
what was out there,

The window of the blacking factory. My feet are stuck in place. They are sticking to the pavement. I want to leave you, Charles – in your misery – in your shame. I understand that what you want is for me to turn and go away, but I cannot leave. My eyes are locked on yours – I cannot move my eyes. You glance down at the bottles as you take up another label, but your eyes – your haunted eyes – come up again. And I see them flinch as they find themselves looking into mine.

To observe the shadow of himself.

Much has happened since you were last here, John. The characters were growing uneasy, John, as I happened to mention before. They were worried – worried about me. The characters love me, John, as much – perhaps more, if it can be so – as I love them. In short – in very few words – in a nutshell, as it were – the characters – as a unit – as a consensus – as a fused-entity, I wish you to understand – suspected that you knew too much of my personal business – my personal experiences – my personal concerns – of my childhood and my adult hopes and fears. They thought – they assumed, John – that I'd been telling you of my life – of the experiences that I had, John, as a boy and in my early years – that have made me into the man that I am today. They feared, John – they feared – I'm merely telling you what they said – that if I put you in a novel – made you a character in a tale – you would reveal the thoughts and emotions – the joys and the agonies, as it were – that they – and I admit it, that they and also I – do not want the reading public ever to know.

He was looking for an avenue –
a broad highway of escape.

Everyone marveled that he worked with such dexterity.

He would don the appropriate clothing
from the cupboard.

Southwark bridge which is of iron.
London bridge which is of stone.
An autumn evening was closing in.

Now I had told them, John, of my plans for a mystery-novel – one whose main character, John, would have been you. I told them that I had been very cautious – very wary – where you were concerned – that I had been extremely discreet, John, but they insisted that I should take further precautions, just the same. They were not afraid of you, John – they were actually afraid of me. They feared that I would write a tale that would blow the lid off my life – break the chain that seals the cabinet – the vault – the monument – of my most secret, most private concerns. They thought – they thought as a body, John – as a unit – a unit of one – as a community of characters, John – that such a literary project – a voyage to uncharted lands – if I were allowed to carry on – if you and I were allowed to proceed, John – would have sailed too close to the rocks along the coastline of my life. The characters felt – to put it bluntly – that I had made an egregious error in creating you.

There seemed no order to these latter visions.

I've always been super-sensitive, John. It's a painful thing to be. One is always taking precautions, without knowing whether they are needed – one wonders – at all.

Every one of them wore chains.

The people came to see what the boy had shouted. Sure enough the water in the river was flowing upstream. All the water that had fallen as rain on the mountains. It was tugging the other way on the fishing line.

Perhaps the boy would grow up to be an author.

"The variety of modes in the presentation of a Dickens narrative makes his novels akin to the poetic drama."

"Complexity of presentation is the wall that Dickens has built between himself and the darkest days of his existence."

Dickens the man and Dickens the boy.

Who is the Dickens who sits in his chair and talks to me?

Half of the book would be printed pages.
All that the reader would need to know.
The second half would be empty pages.
Lying in wait for the reader to fill.

Throw it far out - the idea of you - the only time i know of - no possible consequences - presenting his credentials - a painful part - completely different sphere - a very good question - a separate peal of echoes - quite terribly misspent.

Let it also be borne in mind that Scrooge had not bestowed one thought on Marley, since his last mention of his seven years' dead partner that afternoon. And then let any man explain to me, if he can, how it happened that Scrooge, having his key in the lock of the door, saw in the knocker, without its undergoing any intermediate process of change – not a knocker, but Marley's face.

Marley's face. It was not in impenetrable shadow as the other objects in the yard were, but had a dismal light about it, like a bad lobster in a dark cellar. It was not angry or ferocious, but looked at Scrooge as Marley used to look: with ghostly spectacles turned up on its ghostly forehead.

but a mirror is a glass,
all the same.

The boy – the boy-Dickens – stops working. He looks at me. He seems to be frozen in place. His eyes are filled with all the misery of the world. I try to move my feet. I try to move my tongue. I am sorry, Charles – I think – I say – but he cannot hear. I have no wish to add to your agony. I would help you if I could. I will go away as soon as I am allowed. The boy looks at me – pain and bewilderment fill his eyes. He is wondering, I am sure, what to make of it all. I look at the boy – our eyes are locked – as if they are fused. Am I the boy and is he me? I feel a searing pain as our eyeballs touch. In these eyes are all the agonies of the world.

Separate it from the darkness.

I'd like to thank you, Mr. Dickens, for this experience. It's a very rare privilege, I am sure. My appreciation for what you have shown me knows no bounds. I'm sure you'll understand if I say that some of the elements of this experience have been quite obvious to me, while others will take much time before they are known.

You know, John – a person asked me once – a person asked me a question – a person with a sentimental bent, to be sure. How – this person asked – how – after creating her and living with her – loving her, as I love my family, as I love my friends – I try so hard, John, to love my multiple-restless-selves – how could I love this girl, he asked me – as I was telling him that I, as a novelist, was extremely prone to do – how, he asked, did I have the nerve – the fortitude – the lack of kindness – the iron resolve – the dark necessity, I would say – to – what? – to terminate – to end – to put period – to my character, Little Nell? Well, John – it was hard to explain to this person – in fact, I didn't venture to try. I simply thought to myself – as he assumed, I am sure, that I was ignoring his question – or that I hadn't heard it, perhaps – but I thought – to myself – that a character, John, is created out of necessity – and out of necessity, then, in turn, an author is compelled, sometimes, to cause a character – as was the case on that occasion – to cease – to desist – to depart – John – in short, frankly, to die. Necessity, John – necessity. For life and also for death. Necessity in all we say and all we do. So – sometimes it's a trade-off, John. The death of Little Nell – the life of Tiny Tim. You can't save all of your characters, though you might go to great lengths to try. Sometimes you wonder if you'll be able to save yourself.

The night renewed his strength as he slept on the barren rock.
At daybreak, he considered his chances if he should plunge into the water and swim for shore.

Years went by

A creature asleep in a bog.
A person moving another out of the way.
A completely silent scene.

as the story wandered,

What would you say has been the effect of all that reading?
Would you say that your earliest reading has affected you most?
What is the connection between your reading and your life?

having no success at all.

Well – this seems to be somewhat of an ending – but I don't know whether to feel dead or to feel alive. What, after all, did happen to Edwin Drood? Was he disposed of? – eliminated? – cancelled? – for someone else's gain? – or was he waiting-in-reserve to appear on the scene at some later, more propitious time? – or did he simply go away on a quest of his own? The novel doesn't say that he was murdered, though that's what many readers seem to assume. After all – to coin an aphorism – not every disappearance is a crime.

Secrets that few would care to scrutinize.

All the water that had flowed through the river and down to the lake. All the water that had left the lake and flowed to the sea. Sure enough, the water in the river was flowing upstream. The people wondered whether there would be water to drink.

Chapter 10

Warming up in the car. Fire up the engine and turn on the heater once in a while. Polishing my chapter with the window open a crack. Wouldn't want to suffocate and die in my car.

This consolatory perspective.

Now for the second half of the ritual. Ritual back and ritual forward. Ritual up and ritual down. Every square is a circle – every circle is a square. Every so often each part of the wheel will touch the ground.

The lone and level

A man walking beside a lake.
A boy with blacking on his fingers.
A man scanning a beach for a smooth stone.

sands

What is the point about myth and ritual?
What do they have do to with the living of life?
Do they have any relevance at all?

stretched far away.

An ancient English cathedral tower.

The well-known massive grey square tower.
How can that be here?

I take a break and walk the beach and look for a nice smooth stone. Drifts of snow and chunks of ice today, but plenty of open sand. I take off my glove and pick up a small, smooth stone. I test the smoothness with my fingers and put it in the pocket of my coat. Put my glove back on and look out at the water for a while.
All the mysteries of wonderful creation.
December and Dickens – Dickens and December. What do Dickens and December mean to me?

If so, perhaps he would write about his life.

"In his early novels, Dickens and the reader hold hands, as they walk towards an agreed-upon goal."
"In his later novels, Dickens holds the reader off, at arm's length."

Driving back along the river from the lake.
I could use another coffee against the chill.

The sailor swam
towards the book
as the waves rose higher.

Every memento and keepsake - more than simply air - another race of creatures - a single image - two kindred spirits - thinking of something else - weight of mature awareness - there is some force - watching them in rehearsal - everything will be in motion.

The hair was curiously stirred, as if by breath or

hot air; and, though the eyes were wide open, they were perfectly motionless. That, and its livid colour, made it horrible; but its horror seemed to be in spite of the face and beyond its control, rather than a part of its own expression.

As Scrooge looked fixedly at this phenomenon, it was a knocker again. To say that he was not startled, or that his blood was not conscious of a terrible sensation to which it had been a stranger from infancy, would be untrue. But he put his hand upon the key he had relinquished, turned it sturdily, walked in, and lighted his candle.

so he spent his life
on the dark side
of the moon.

I get in the car and fire up the engine – turn up the heater and drive away. The tires crunch over the stones in the parking lot. Out on the road and into the half-hour drive back home.
The same ray of sunlight.
In time, under the water, that jagged stone will be worn smooth by the action of the sand and the ebb and flow. It will be both the-same and not-the-same stone.

He felt the gloom of the gossiping houses
closing in.

There was blacking on his fingers as he worked.

Then he would straighten his shoulders
and open up the door.

No spike of rusty iron.
In the air between the eye and it.
From any point of the real prospect.

Yes – the sun is up and shining. I left home at the break of dawn. Love the sun as it sparkles and dances on the clean, white snow.

Wise enough to know.

December and Dickens – Dickens and December. Thoughts of Dickens and December just won't go away. Dickens sleeps and keeps his secrets. No one has ever solved the mystery of Edwin Drood.

No fog, no mist, clear, bright, jovial, stirring, cold.

The second part of the ritual is just as important as the first – much easier at Easter and Thanksgiving – or at one or two special birthdays throughout the year. No trouble, today, on the wind-swept beach, to find a smooth stone.

If so, perhaps he would write about his life.

"A Dickens novel is not an easy novel to read."

"A Dickens novel makes an unrelenting demand on the reader's attention."

Driving back to the house and wood-lot near Cayuga.

I'll buy a muffin for my wife at the coffee shop.

The sailor clung
to the book
throughout the storm.

Everything about him - one needs a spark - around the outer-edges - an organ of perception - their useful course - your deepest experiences - would not be involved - the power of control - torches leading the way - piled up on the shore.

He did pause, with a moment's irresolution, before he shut the door; and he did look cautiously behind it first, as if he half expected to be terrified with the sight of Marley's pigtail sticking out into the hall. But there was nothing on the back of the door, except the screws and nuts that held the knocker on, so he said "Pooh, pooh!" and closed it with a bang.

The sound resounded through the house like thunder. Every room above, and every cask in the wine-merchant's cellars below, appeared to have a separate peal of echoes of its own. Scrooge was not a man to be frightened by echoes. He fastened the door, and walked across the hall, and up the stairs; slowly too: trimming his candle as he went.

Unless it's broken –
then you'd say
it's neither one.

Snow in the fields and the roads are clear. The perfect winter weather. Ice in patches along the river with stretches bare. Not a very cold December after all.
Overthrows the brain and breaks the heart.
There's just one lingering question. What would have happened to the Dickens-characters if he hadn't written the book, and we didn't have *A Christmas Carol* to read?

The story wondered

A man performing a ritual.
A novel which is not easy to read.
A part of a wheel touching the ground.

whether its tale

What is the significance of the ritual that you have created?
Why throw a jagged stone into the lake?
Why search the windy beach for a smooth stone?

would ever be told.

Snow on the fields but the roads are bare. Milder weather all over the earth, these days, so they say. In the old days we would skate from October to March. I'll toss the smooth stone into our pond when I get home.
God bless us every one.
My wife will be working on the decorating all day. She works on one room at a time. The house is completely transformed at Christmas time. I'll carry the empty boxes back downstairs and put them on their shelves. Then come the end of January, she'll change the whole house back again. Then comes Valentine's and Easter and Thanksgiving. The enchantment of the seasons as the year moves on.

Three Books

John and Dickens: A Christmas Mystery – a novel
One morning in December, the writer, John Passfield, leaves his home, buys a coffee and drives down to Lake Erie to perform a Christmas ritual that he has developed over the years. Suddenly, he finds himself in the writing-room of Charles Dickens, who explains his new idea for a Christmas tale. Dickens invites John to watch rehearsals for the writing of the story, but as Dickens struggles through contentious negotiations with his amazingly independent characters, John wonders whether *A Christmas Carol* will ever be written.

The Making of John and Dickens: A Christmas Mystery – a reflective journal
This journal records the author's reflections on the process of the crafting of the novel as it evolved through the stages of planning, writing, editing and polishing. It constitutes an effort to be as conscious as possible of the process whereby the single idea that suggested the topic of the novel was expanded into a complex work of art. Topics range from the nuts and bolts of novel-building to the nature of the novel as an art-form.

Planning John and Dickens: A Christmas Mystery
– a planning notebook

During the writing of the novel, the author kept a notebook which records the day-by-day development of the novel as it found its shape and style. The notebook reveals how a vast cluster of thoughts was sifted, selected, structured and polished into novel-form.

The Project

Together, this novel, journal and notebook comprise the thirty-second installment in an on-going novel-writing project in which the author is exploring the concept of form and meaning in the novel, and of the novel as a form of expression in the 21st century. All of the published journals and notebooks are available for free download at www.johnpassfield.ca.

About the Author

John Passfield was born in St. Thomas, Ontario, Canada, and continues to reside in Southern Ontario, near Cayuga, with his family. He is interested in exploring the development of the novel as an art-form in a search for a form for the poetic novel of our time. He has published almost thirty novels, and his planning notebooks and journals are available for free access on his website, johnpassfield.ca. His novel *John Passfield: Saturday Morning* was shortlisted for the ReLit award in 2022. He has posted more than one hundred readings on YouTube, each of which presents a passage from one of his novels and a comment on an aspect of the craft of novel-writing.

Novels by John Passfield

Grave Song
The Agony of Robert Chisholm

Jumbo
P. T. Barnum's Greatest Creation

Pinafore Park
The Swan Boat Incident

Water Lane
The Pilgrimage of Christopher Marlowe

Rain of Fire
The Ordeal of Conductor Spettigue

Victoria Day
The Fabric of the Community

The Wright Brothers
Flight is Possible

Leni Riefenstahl
The Valley of the Shadow

Out of the Park
The Cogitations of Babe Ruth

Raskolnikov
Murder with an Axe

Death Day
The Apology of Sergei Eisenstein

Einstein
Wonder

Geoffrey Chaucer
Canterbury Bound

Ospringe
A Visit with Grandad

Pompeii
Vesuvius Dominus

Beethoven
The Ninth Immersion

Job
The Cornerstone of the Universe

Bethune
The Only Person Alive in the World

Terry Fox
Somewhere the Hurting Must Stop

Lord and Lady Macbeth
Full of Scorpions is My Mind

Cyril Passfield
Out West

Glenn Gould
Light and Dark

Emily Brontë
More Myself Than I

L. M. Montgomery
I Gave You Life

Pauline Johnson
Know Who I Am

John Passfield
Saturday Morning

Eleonora Duse
Let Me Have My Wings

James McIntyre
The Mammoth Cheese

Shakespeare and Cleopatra
My Life Is Not My Own

John and Santa
The Cowboy Shirt

John and Cassandra
Fair is Fair

John and Dickens
A Christmas Mystery

John and Lewis Carroll
Wonder Fall

John and Mother Goose
The Carnival of Tales

See www.johnpassfield.ca for publishing information.

In Search of Form and Meaning: Journals by John Passfield

Each journal is a day-by-day record of the complex process that a writer undergoes while crafting a work of art. It records the largest decisions, of structure and theme, and the smallest decisions, such as the choice of one word over another, and the constant interaction between the two. Each journal is a record of a writer's reflection on the craft of novel-writing.

The Making of Grave Song

The Making of Jumbo

The Making of Pinafore Park

The Making of Water Lane

The Making of Rain of Fire

The Making of Victoria Day

The Making of Flight is Possible

The Making of The Valley of the Shadow

The Making of Out of the Park

The Making of Murder with an Axe

The Making of Death Day

The Making of Wonder

The Making of Canterbury Bound

The Making of Ospringe

The Making of Vesuvius Dominus

The Making of The Ninth Immersion

The Making of The Cornerstone of the Universe

The Making of The Only Person Alive in the World

The Making of Somewhere the Hurting Must Stop

The Making of Full of Scorpions is My Mind

The Making of Out West

The Making of Glenn Gould: Light and Dark

The Making of Emily Brontë: More Myself Than I

The Making of L. M. Montgomery: I Gave You Life

The Making of Pauline Johnson: Know Who I Am

The Making of John Passfield: Saturday Morning

The Making of Eleonora Duse: Let Me Have My
Wings

The Making of James McIntyre: The Mammoth
Cheese

The Making of Shakespeare and Cleopatra: My Life Is
Not My Own

The Making of John and Santa: The Cowboy Shirt

The Making of John and Cassandra: Fair is Fair

The Making of John and Dickens: A Christmas
Mystery

The Making of John and Lewis Carroll: Wonder Fall

The Making of John and Mother Goose: The Carnival
of Tales

See www.johnpassfield.ca for free access.

The Novel as an Art-Form:
Planning Notebooks
by John Passfield

Each planning notebook records the planning, writing, editing and polishing of each novel. Each notebook is an attempt to understand and organize the vast cluster of thoughts which occur as one grapples with the various levels of organization which a clear yet complex work of art demands.

Planning Grave Song

Planning Jumbo

Planning Pinafore Park

Planning Water Lane

Planning Rain of Fire

Planning Victoria Day

Planning Flight is Possible

Planning The Valley of the Shadow

Planning Out of the Park

Planning Murder with an Axe

Planning Death Day

Planning Wonder

Planning Canterbury Bound

Planning Ospringe

Planning Vesuvius Dominus

Planning The Ninth Immersion

Planning The Cornerstone of the Universe

Planning The Only Person Alive in the World

Planning Somewhere the Hurting Must Stop

Planning Full of Scorpions is My Mind

Planning Out West

Planning Glenn Gould: Light and Dark

Planning Emily Brontë: More Myself Than I

Planning L. M. Montgomery: I Gave You Life

Planning Pauline Johnson: Know Who I Am

Planning John Passfield: Saturday Morning

Planning Eleonora Duse: Let Me Have My Wings

Planning James McIntyre: The Mammoth Cheese

Planning Shakespeare and Cleopatra: My Life Is Not My Own

Planning John and Santa: The Cowboy Shirt

Planning John and Cassandra: Fair is Fair

Planning John and Dickens: A Christmas Mystery

Planning John and Lewis Carroll: Wonder Fall

Planning John and Mother Goose: The Carnival of Tales

See www.johnpassfield.ca for free access.